AF010393

NIGHT OF THE WORLD 2

By Oscar Guardiola-Rivera

Published 2024 by the87press
The 87 Press LTD
87 Stonecot Hill
Sutton
Surrey
SM3 9HJ
www.the87press.co.uk

Under the World: Night of the World 2
© Oscar Guardiola-Rivera, 2024

The moral right of Oscar Guardiola-Rivera has been asserted in accordance with the Copyright, Designs and Patents Act 1988

ISBN: 978-1-7393939-7-7

Printed and bound by CPI Group (UK) Ltd, Croydon, CR0 4YY
Cover image: #bajas IV by Greta Chicheri (2013) with the author's permission.
Design: Stanislava Stoilova [www.sdesign.graphics]

Inspired by the Mayan Book of the Dawn of Life,
Popol Vuh

Contents

Prologue	1
Episode 1. In the Dark	5
Episode 2. Down in a Hole	61
Episode 3. Standoff	113
Epilogue	167

Prologue

This manuscript may be read
as a roots rave manifesto
to free literature,
its wider space
its dark matter,
of memory and theatre.

An invitation
to make a sideways move,
dance and turn
to re-turn
from the absolute reign of
linear composition
in novels and linear narratives,
to the plebeian
texts
of image, object, and sound
that can be found
throughout the native Americas.

The tree, the trunk, and the roots,
the past-future,
to which we're bound.

Looking forwards,
to futures past,
we move backwards.

To envision an inhabitable future,
perhaps we would do well
to find a rock crevice,

an entry
into the underground,
and go backward.

To find our roots,
perhaps we would do well
looking for them where roots are usually found.

It is as she says,
the seer of this tale:

"At least the Spirit of Place
is a more benign one
than the exclusive
and aggressive
Spirit of Race."[1]

This is an invitation provocation.

To call for a revolution
in the kingdom of plot,
which is no longer a lighthouse,
but a wreckers' lantern
luring us aground

in the **night of the world**

to loot us.

This is also a tale,

---

[1] Ursula K. Le Guin, "A Non-Euclidean View of California as a Cold Place to Be," in Thomas More's *Utopia*, intr. by China Miéville with essays by U. K. Le Guin (London: Verso, 2016) 171-2.

or the discontinuity of a tale
told in the old form of a katabasis.
About what happened to Hoodoo Girl
after she fought an inquisitor witch
at sea
and trapped hope,
a trickster named Ix,
who may or may not be her sister and lover,
to see
the new day
in the bottom of a jar.

Where is she/they?

Like the rest of us.
In the dark.

Episode 1. In the Dark

I Am ~~Not~~ Here

I am ~~not~~ here.
I could ~~not~~ be.
Do ~~not~~ ask my name.

For I lost it the same night
I lost
my crew
my friends
my mirror and soul.
The same night
I turned,
or returned,
backwards in time.
Do not ask for my story.
It isn't as if I have forgotten who I am
or what my story is.
(Perhaps I have)
More truthful it would be
for you to figure
(out/down & out)
what is like
to be conscripted into
History
as I was.
By negation,
Backwards,
upside down,
and falling downwards.
Disinherited from a past
that was never properly ours,
displaced
violated

from behind.
Damned,
Condemned
to be out of place
brought to a phantom place
where history never took place
As it should.
My story is a bad story.
A wayward story.
It organised
my family story,
our inner lives.
"This waywardness
Organized our inner lives."[2]
It's the same with all of us,
the people of Caliban.
We were displaced,
brought from somewhere else into this
nowhere place,
without beginning or a tall tale of origins
to call our own,
dispossessed of a history
that was never ours in the first place.
So, do ~~not~~ ask what happened to me.
I've told you already.
I was at sea. Unable to see
for I had lost my mirror and soul.
That is why now
I have no precise way
of collecting in a tight line & plot
the chain of causes or agency

---

[2] Stuart Hall with Bill Schwarz, *Familiar Stranger. A Life Between Two Islands* (London: Penguin, 2017) 61.

that brought me here.
I have
No pedantic way.
No precise way.
No linear method
to bring the pieces together
in a manner that would make sense
to someone looking from afar,
standing on the firmest land,
assuming that a recollection,
most precise,
would be the same
as having the experience I've had.

Plot is overrated.
Plot is the suppressed fire
of Quetzalcoatl's
Dark Mirror.
(Suppressed rhythms
and music as well).

Music in text is
synchronous
with incandescent imagination.

A Perfect Day

Let me put it otherwise.
Pick a day.
Any day.
It's a beautiful day.
A perfect day.
You wish you could relieve it.
What if you could?
It would be like having
a perfect recording device,
a video device,
able not only to store
every visual impulse caught between

> your eyelid
> and the centre of your eye
> but in the centre of your eye
> every moment

every timbre of every sound
every beat pounding your chest
so you scream aloud
every whiff of every smell and
every last vibration
of every last touch and sound.

Wouldn't you jump at the chance of reliving
every select moment of your life?

That's what the Inquisitor,
his witches and priests promised us.

Utopia.

An Euclidean one.

A perfect replay.
A forever replay.
A mirror-soul replay.

A mirror-soul was such a perfect device, an
AI device.

And yet, such a thing would ~~erase~~ its very sense
of being a replay in the first place.

      Because it would erase the connection
          between

the moments of time you lived   and the very act of
             you remembering them.

No self, then.   And no other, then.

     Because there would be no
now   and   then.

What about love, then?

We love because,
and only because,
we can lose what we love.

It hurts.
I should know.
After all,

I lost the one I loved.
I lost my mother & father.
I lost my friends
in the last bombardment.

But I rather live the next five centuries in pain
than never to have fallen in love,

                                          in
                                          the
                                          first place.

At least
the Spirit of Place
is a more benign one
than the Spirit of Race.

This Wouldn't Be a Story

This wouldn't be a story
if it had
no now
and
no then.
No beginning and no end.
But let us not confuse that with reason and its unfolding.
Nor with matter,
otherwise inert,
and its formation after a fashion, an order, or an intention.
All
    I
        have
             is
                frag
                    ments.
Scattered p-i-e-c-e-s.
Sound samplings.
Beats,
bits of a broken mirror.

Memories,
moments,
and events.

Back then there was me.
I was her, my back against the wall,
pinned to the floor of a council state flat in ExLondon
by police
and an inquisition witch
for being a bitch

to my mother
and not following their manners and creeds.
For listening to abuela
her fanciful stories
and to Bowie.

For being visited by the ghost of my father,
and falling in love with a Muslim neighbour.

They disliked my listening to black music.
And, most of all, my reading books,
which were forbidden,
Replaced by downloads.

They pinned me down.
So, I lit a fire within me.
The suppressed fire
of a dark mirror
                        In sync
with rhythm & music,
                        In sync
with incandescent imagination.

I lit
a dark flame,
an all-consuming fire.
And then I ran,
I ran like hell.

Took a Muslim sister with me.
I loved her.

At the river port, we said our farewells.
"I'll find you, in whatever form, one day,"

she said.

But I lost her.
When I took to sea.
To see.
Foresee to really see.
What they don't want us to see.

Or was it the other way around,
to unsee?

In the end,
an end I couldn't foresee,
the witch came after me and her
and all our friends.

Unleashed a mighty beast, made of subtle vapour,
or air.

She worked for the Great Inquisitor,
that bitch,
in the Home Office.

They say
"tru$t u$"
But they wish
to break us
kill us
hate us.

To take from us the elements
of story
stored
in the cargo bay of our ship at sea,

which we were taking across the ocean sea
to the free people of the library at The Garden
for them to free themselves
To see and tell stories again.

Liberation.

That is the goal
Such is the aim,
still.

Tell? I cannot tell, for we have lost the elements of story.
They were taken by the witch.
Where?
I cannot see.
I've lost my sister, my love,
my friends,
my mirror & soul.

Perhaps also my imagination
and the will to live.

It all happened one night.
The night of the world.

They came.
Took us by surprise. Put us under siege,
fired their missiles,
at our homes,
our schools,
and our hospitals.

Said it was in self-defence.

And all the media said the same.

I lost my eyes & sense.

When I came to consciousness again,
I was stranded at sea,
alone,
unseen.

My friends, my name, my mirror and soul were
nowhere to be seen.

So, please.
Do ~~not~~ ask my name. For there's
no word for it.
Do not ask for my story.
It hasn't happened yet.
Do not ask what happened to me.
I can't tell you.
Not yet.
Ask, instead,
where do words,
and tricksters,
and djinns,
and girls
that can light fires like me,
where do they come from?

Where do I have to go
to find the elements from which stories are made?

To allow for the return
 of the sunlight
of the tales

of survivance
to the heart of the sun
for it to shine upon this world
and her moon
now in darkness and despair.

"Hope is a thing with feathers,"
my father used to say,
repeating the words of a forgotten poet.
But it is worse.
Hope is trapped in a jar,
in the dark.
So that's where I will start.
Where all stories start.

In the dark.

Things to be Found in the Dark

Isolation.
Loneliness.
Desolation.
Blood and the things of blood.
Animals acting like men.
Such as trickster Crow & Raven.
That boygirl makes the world.
Men acting like animals.
Such as Coyote, the Djinn,
or Compay Anansi,
the spider,
who can web stories & shape-shift,
and girls who light fires.

Memories not monuments.

These are the things to be found in the dark.

Story of Hu

I

Llegó aquí entonces la palabra.
Tepeu, the Crow,
and Gucumetz, a shape-shifting Coyote,
sometimes a Spider,
came together in the dark of night.
They spoke in pictures
for words had not been created yet.
Dwelling on the matter
they agreed to bring together
their thought
and the sounds
Of heart & breathing.

Thus, storytelling began.

The relation of relations
of how everything that was in suspension
never was
because nothing ever is in suspension
and never has been in such a state of negation
all still
all silent
all quiet
for there's no such thing as
empty extension and therefore
no caves & no holes on the surface of the earth
or at the bottom of the sea.
No animals over it
or beneath it.

No fish
no jaguars or tigers
no stones or trees.
No manifestation of the face of the earth.

Sólo el pájaro de fuego que vuela sobre el mar del ahora y el después y lo observa.

Only the sea of Crow's thought and Coyote's sky sound.

Nothing was related to anything in itself
but to something else.
So, there's nothing in itself
standing still on its quiet own being.

The bird flies over the water
rolling backwards in parts and beats at times
jumping from parts to axion waves
that reverb saturate
the music scale
without repetition or delay
without anything moving in between
only cut-in and overlay.

It carries Tepeu and Gucumetz,
in the sense that movement
is not something that happens to gods,
humans,
or things,
but rather,
gods,
humans,
and all things,
down to their innermost parts or beats

are something derived
from our observations of movement.

It doesn't mean they do not exist.

In the water
rolling backwards in parts and beats,
at times surrounded by the dark,
Tepeu and Gucumetz observed a great commotion.
A trickster djinn
in battle with a girl
who had no name
being trapped in a jar.
A witch fleeing the scene
with the things that can only be found in the dark.
She opened a hole at the bottom of the sea
onto the other side,
the backroom side,
the not-yet side.

Tepeu and Gucumetz saw this
through the eyes of the bird of before times.
Which was the only thing that could be observed
and observe in the dark
because of its silver eyes
and the splendour of its green and blue plumage.

Quetzal.

II

Tepeu and Gucumetz are called mother and father.
They are rolled into one.

Their nature is that of thought and rhythm sound.

This is how the sky came to be.
But also, the heart of the sky.

They wondered:
How can this be?
How can we tell the others
what we have seen
if there are no words still
and the witch has hidden in a hole in the dark
all the things that can be found in the dark?

So, they decided to weave together
Crow's thought and Coyote's sound
and this is how the word came to be.

The living word.
The heart of the sky.

No manifestation or destiny.
But
worlding word
or figuration.

A memory
coming from the same subtle matter
that girls who can light fires are made of.

Una mujer de maíz.

She will face the dark
and the heart of the dark
and in the dark of night

she will fight death itself
to return the elements of story
for the coming of another_kind.

This is no manifestation,
but the worlding & figuration
of Tepeu and Gucumetz,
which is always incomplete
and must be reanimated
time and time again
which must be rendered into music & song
for it to be sung
so that time can continue to exist
and for worlds to exist

In time.
Of time.
Against the times.

And for all to know
that her name is incomplete,
but not lost.

And she's now called Huracán.

El país de la penumbra

This is the journey of Hu girl to the land of the dead.

A memory of how she brought back

                the gift of the storier.

For stories themselves come from darkness.
They are gifts from the dead.

She was born
you might recall
with the gift of fire
at a time when light
had been robbed

                from the world

and the first men drowned.

The skies were cold
The sun hid underground
obscured by gas clouds
the cities doomed and domed
covered the faces of the moon and the sun
drowned the men of clay and wood.

In this world,
Vucub Caquix ruled
over the few places
spared by the great heat and deluge.

Of silver were his eyes
shining dark like obsidian mirrors
                              without light
                              capturing the souls
                              of the drowned
                              to adorn his teeth.

He would send an inquisitor witch
to rob Hodoo Girl of her name,
the land of ancestors,
her mirror and soul,
for his ambition was to swallow all others
                              in his being.

Then came the word,
a figuration and worlding of Coyote and Crow,
in the drowned world,
and with it the girl.

The girl that lit a fire.

Having survived
having lost her mirror and soul
she renamed herself
Hu/Huracán/Hunah pú.

She was the first.

The second,
made of the same subtle matter
words
and firegirls
are made of,
we shall call Ix or /x/

Ixbalanqué.

As in Latinx
Or Malcolm X.

Trapped inside a jar,
Ix was washed up
on a beach
in an unknown coast
on the other side of the sea.
Found a fire kin,
Coyote
who shape-shifting into a feathered serpent
took the jar
(from the white witch)
down into a cave
at the entrance of hell
into the place they call The Backroom
so that it could be found by Hu girl.

Hoodoo Girl
Hu
now
Huracán,
fallen feather of a firebird,
drifted at sea.
She was washed up
on a beach
in an unknown coast
on the other side of the sea.
Found a fire kin,
Crow,
who once flew
with the chariot of the sun,

he's the harbinger of healing
heatwaves
and axion waves

The lowest rhythmic interval
becoming music or wave.
An axion mass scale wave.
It acts
sometimes
as if made of billiard-ball parts
and other times
sloshing like watery waves.
Waves coming together in rhythmic overlay
to create a super wave
that no archive can place
in a final resting place.

Crow spoke to Hu
the only way he can.
He
spoke in pictures,
of the healing that could only be found by a girl
     down underground
and of the things that only in the underworld
     can be found.

Here. Now. I am here.
Hu said,
as she moved backwards
into the cave
    downwards
into the land they call Xibalbá.
The Land of the Dead.
El País de las Masacres.
El País de la Penumbra.

Story of All Stories

Everyone knows that
djinn,
tricksters,
and girls
are made of **sub**tle fire.

A **sub**terranean incandescence,
simultaneous
with image

        &

                the rhythm of a beat.

                No longer a **sub**stitute metaphor
                But the bract which **sub**tends
                And enfolds all literature.

No one knows where such matter came from.

How it came to be

                superpositioned

                                      and

                intertwined

in the atom heart
of djinn and girls with exploding hearts.

Suppose it's subterranean.

I mean,
how they made a secret pact

to go down underground
moving sdrawkcab and
d
 o
  w
   n
    w
     a
      r
       d
        s
to defeat the lord of death
hidden in the dark
and bring back light,
a **trans**itive medium,
between heaven and sky.

Music/makers whistling
through a window,
located in a corridor,
in Lord Death's palace,
in ancient El Dorado,
subbed darkness for
the wind sound of a whistle
or the skin sound of the pound drum
that in such an instant becomes,
a secret medium of **trans**itive density.

I emphasise **trans**, **subt**leness, and **density**.
As though a beat or a chord
exists within that window,
the window that goes down & out
-within the density of the window (let us say)

and the skin of a drum.
So, the window,
located in a corridor,
in Lord Death's palace,
in ancient Xibalbá or El Dorado,
becomes a medium of transitive density
as the chord & the beat fire,
(so)
to speak,
and their whistle is transformed
as it passes through the window
into an eruption of
Fantastic
Critique & disruption
light & music
that lives
within the heart of subtle things.
Such as word,
wind,
whistle,
downward bound
through a cave or a window
and into the text of reality.

It fires,
the word fires,
in sync with the music & the beat.

And thus appears,
in sync with the beat & the music,
the lightning bract
That subtends the flower and bark of a tree.

It is the flower, the tree, and the trunk

of Continental Liberty.
The long continental
literary tradition
of literature in the Americas.

Such tribal literatures are the tree,
the oldest literatures.
They *are* the canon.
But we don't see the tree,
because the things of **sub**tle density
at its root
remain obscured
by an idea of
Order
&
Exhibition
&
Publication,
the logic of the museum & the archive,
in which everything would have
its final resting place
or no place at all.

Such was/is
the utopia
of the Big Inquisitor
and his witch in the Home Office.

But in the atom heart
of djinn and girls with exploding hearts
there is an alliance.

An old alliance
between music & text.

As old as the tradition of
Continental Liberty.

Which is simultaneous
with the incandescent imagination
With which all the stories are made.

This is their story.
The story of that alliance.
The alliance between a djinn and a girl.
Hu & Ix.
And of how
they went underground,
to bring back the exploding sun of stories.

If so,
it is also
the story
of all the stories that have ever been made.

A feather
from the bird of before times
&
from the bird of after times
falling from the straight line.

A declining clinamen.

A bass beat at the top of the song.

Beat. Beat. Beat.

T...
    ...th

...the

There was, back
                       then
no light over the face of the earth.

There was no sun.
Only the night of the world.

And no word
only the thought of Crow
and the shape-shifting music sound of Coyote beat
which
he cuts-in and overlays
at random
in his midi mixing machine
to make mighty mountains
of
magma
       move

                sideways,
backwards

and
↓
  downwards

where worlds wane and wither,
worlds woven,
winds wandering wildly
until the girl who fell from the straight line,
in declining clinamen,
like the bass beat at the top of a song,

comes to let understanding stop
at what cannot be understood.

An incandescent sky,
in sync with the imagination,
wound and unwound,
would then
shine again.

But there was also a being,
a vain,
       and **vain**glorious
being
named Vucub Caquix

                            el pájaro de fuego
                            a firebird

hovering high over the heavens
        high over the holes

                            that molten magma
                            coming from the feathers
                            of the firebird

had left

                            while it crossed between
                            now and then.

It all happened after the first men drowned.
When the face of the world was covered,
and the face of the sun was covered,
and the face of the moon was covered.

And darkness reigned all around.

Vucub Caquix said:

"Truly, there were only the men who drowned.
Now I will be great and grand and master
over/all that is left.
To me they will be bound.
Those ascending the stare
between my eyelid and the centre of my eye,
and those gone underground.
Those who already are,
and those who are but not yet.
For I will replace the shine of the Sun and the Moon
with the green and blue splendour of my plumage
quetzal.

Of slithering silver are my eyes
shining and shivering in the dark,
like emeralds.
They can see from Yucatán to Transvaal,
like the mirrors without light that captured the souls of the
drowned.
My teeth encased in gold and diamonds.
My wings and body bright from afar,
like the Sun
and the Moon
made of fire,
they can turn all into ash.
Great is the extension of my sight,
and greater still is the illuminating distance of the light
coming into my silvery eyes."

So said the bird of fire,
even though his sight could only extend to the horizon line,
projected onto the imaginary divide between heaven and the
earth.
The earth

that looks flat from where the bird was.

The firebird was ambitious.
He believed his sight could extend over the night of the world.
He believed he could swell the world,
with his own being.

That is why
he is to be killed
by the twins
Hu & Ix
whose very essence emerged
out of the subtle matter
that the universe
and the feathers of the bird
are made of
light & sound
waves and particles
not words
but pebbles of w-o-r-d-s

                          and

                                       syl-la-bles

not letters but fragments of
l
e
t
t
e
r
s
falling like feathers
in declining clinamen
or the subtle matter beyond atoms
and in the spaces between them.

as in JNN
جَنْ or نْجِ
which means to hide,
to be made invisible,
beyond the vanished point of perspective and sight.

Banished to the dark.

It means to change or adapt.
And refers also to what has been hidden down underground
or at the bottom of a jar.
So, to reveal it,
bring it to the light,
the participant observer must invent
A different way of seeing.

A different figuration
a worlding
an image-system
capable of
        sensing
        and making sense
                otherwise.

Not a method or its reason
but a utopia that doesn't look like one.

The trick is
to think what you sense
    &
to sense what you think.

Such is the way.
There's no magic in it

but simple decency
inherited by those who descent from frag
ments
of history,
not from judgmental
statements,
but rather,
from
stammerings,
stone stamens of ruined monuments,
staggermoments
of subtle matter
before words or solemn speeches   before heroic tales or novels
could be said or performed   could be put on a page
       and in the space between them
       where can be found the signs of the possessed
بـوتـچه   majnún
on the other side of
janna   هٔنّجِ،
which is The Garden
    and
چذسذ   janín
which is the unborn,
       unhatched,
unfinished and incomplete becoming.

Life in its early stages,
the life of the word
before words or solemn speeches could be said
or performed.
Before heroic tales or novels could be put on a page,
performed no longer on a stage
but in the stage of the readers' mind
       and in the space between words

                              which is the night of the world
out of which the life-giving,
wind-rising,
storm-riding,
fire-starting
girl named Hurricane
emerged into this world,
together with the jinn,
and made a pact
to help women and men be reborn from maize
Together with their animals,
with birds and jaguars,
who carry in their backs the sun of the night,
composed of a sheath and a long distal blade
joined together by an auricle
so that the blade can bend away

                                            from the stem,
                                            change or adapt
                                            to a hurricane
                                            or a mighty rain.

Such was the secret pact
made
between the jinn and the girl.
Ginnaya and Jaini.
Who will become lovers, sisters, or twins,
Hu and Ix,
Hurricane and Sex.

Memory & Sex

This is the story of their pact.
A lovers' pact.

This is the story of the ruin
of the Lords of Xibalbá
in
the dark place.
And of the fall of Vucub Caquix
at the hands of two sisters,
twins,
or lovers.

Hu   the girl
              and
Ix   the jinn

                            Hurricane   and   Sex

Who were truly godly,
for they were subtle matter.
The pebbles of words
with which to sense and make sense
in a way that no clever device
made by men can
not yet
because to sense and make sense
is to differentiate
between the rules applied to a case
and that which is the case,
the experience of coming to be,
of the world,

and of the life of the word
outside those rules.

Before words and solemn speeches could be performed
alone and isolated
to persuade foot soldiers to carry out
the Inquisitor's command of
blood and the things of blood
and bring displacement and desolation
during the apotheosis of war.

Before heroic stories and novels could be put on a page
                                                                                     sold
and performed in the mind of a reader
isolated
alone
in a desolate place
trying to escape blood and the things of blood
(el país de las masacres, este país)
where animals act as men
men act like animals
and the things that can be found in the dark
are no longer
                                                told
but drenched in blood
to sustain the reign of terror
and maintain the sovereignty
of wealth & riches.

This is the story of our ruin and fall.

And of a pact
made many moons ago

how many
no one knows
between a girl and a jinn
to snatch those things
from the Dark Lords.

This is also a memory,
and like all memories
you wish you could relive it
exactly as it was
only you can't
because reliving that memory
exactly as it was
would mean ~~erasing~~
the difference that permits it
to be a memory
of what it was.

So, this is the story
and the memory
of the subtle matter
that permits
the existence of memory and story.

Trans

I

A subtle matter
A difference only.

A small difference
between the memory of a day
any day
a perfect day
the one you wish you could relive it
and the lived experience
to contrast it.

A small difference.
But one that makes
all the difference

between us and the clever machines we make
between the pedantic precision of rules
their application
by those who claim praetorian,
inquisitorial status
those who wish to swell the world
with their own being
to the point of proclaiming
the repetition of a scene of the past
exhaustive of any novelty to come.
To the point of proclaiming
the security of the burrow
and its stillness paramount.

Let's call that precision forensic, on the one hand.

On the other hand,
the suspension of that forensic proclamation.
And of the inquisitor's judgment.
At the abarian point between field forces,
which appears
in the space created
by breaking apart
the precedents and orders
given by those who burn crosses,
in the name of securing the mole's burrow.
Fantastic precision,
We call it.

Fantastic precision
of the suspension (of judgment)
of hesitation (when the order to kill is given).
To stop the chain of their commands.
To push back against their inertia.

And save lives in the process.

Those who burn crosses
practise a magic
that isn't memorial,
neither music nor the shaman's performance art.
But a monument,
pacifying in its stillness.
Ineffectual
re
presentation
of the sacrifice
of an animal acting as man

a goat
or a lamb
a burrow perhaps.

Those who burn crosses
declare that instant a hinging moment,
the key moment,
the instant in which fate,
dead set in the past,
becomes manifest,
and bears being repeated,
again and again,
for all time.

Again, for all time,
is the same as
the stillness of the burrow.
The joy of the burrow.
The pleasure of the burrow.
The happiness of the burrow which
is the same as
the joy procured by burrowing.
The pure joy afforded by moments of
pure silence and stillness.
Death.
The sheer pleasure of watching
still images projected in the mind,
without music or dance,
and the infinite pleasure
of keeping watch over the burrow's entrance.
So, no foreign stranger can come here.
Contain them
Keep them at bay
Exterminate all the brutes!

Such is the command
of those
that work forces
The same ones who burn crosses
The same who find infinite pleasure
Keeping watch over the burrow's entrance.

They say:

freude
glück
genießen
arbeit macht frei

II

We refuse to.
We revolt against their command.
Their imitation of motion.

If that imitation of motion
exhausts novelty,
the alternate voice & sound   (Coyote)
of an alternative thought   (Crow)
becoming beat & voice
       rhythm & song
       music & dance,
then its message is
one of death:
don't move
don't take apart
don't doubt or criticise
don't refuse
don't dare to hesitate, change, or revolt.

And its happiness
the stillness of
what just is.
The belief that work
shall set you free.

We are led astray here.
To confuse what just is with justice.
That confusion paves the way to the camps
and the killing fields
of the apotheosis of war in the lands of our childhood.

No motion,
no sub,
no beat,
no trans.

Such dark magical worldview
is the point of spectacle.
And of the world,
the night of the world,
in which we live now.

A world
inherited from the Fourth Lateran Council,
and the feast day of the Eucharist.
Imprinted upon us
every Sunday of childhood.
When we were told
that the communion wafer, when blessed,
comes back as the body
of an animal acting as man
a goat
or a lamb

perhaps a burrow.

It matters not whether you believe or not
(that)
such a thing is possible.
The point is not
faith or belief.

But the fact that we are called upon
to act
as if we still believed.

For no one believes today
in the same way
the crowds of Liège rushed to witness the elevation
of the Host
by Urban IV in 1264.
For them it was not a matter
of letting yourself go,
or taking a leap of faith,
as they say today.
For them it was a matter of reality.

It is different for us.

If for us
reality has become spectacle.
If in the dark
shadows have come alive.
It is because
the thing called Evil
has come back as a new problem.
We no longer believe in it,
but we feel anxious to let go of our crouches,

grow up,
stare into the abyss,
enter the burrow,
and dare to
go down underground.

So, we prefer to act as if we still believed
in such things as Good or Evil,
and the flames of Hell,
so far as we do not have to enter or experience it.

We prefer to act as if we still believed
in the apotheosis of the Host
so far as we do not have to experience
the apotheosis of war in the lands of their childhood,
so far as we do not have to entertain the memory
or what it was like to be a child,
a boy or a girl,
back then,
when the paras came,
and the basketball field
became hell.
The site of a massacre.

So far as blood and the things of blood
remain in the dark,
buried underground,
under a pyramid of corpses,
in the mass graves of my childhood.

I would have to transform, then.
First into a donkey or a camel.
Then into a lion.
Finally, into a child.

To dream up new domains
and other beginnings.

To fight those who adjudge history in the as if way.
The monumental historians,
who still write as if all the Evil in the world
was the result of a few Evil Men,
and the result of the indifference
of the fewer Good Ones.
Who failed to act in the critical instant.
Who failed to measure in that instant
and to understand
what cannot be measured or understood.
Motion or change in an event,
or a thing as it is in itself.

The monumental historians
who still write as if
we could sense and make sense
or control
the forces at play
in an instant of change
pass judgment
on that September day
when bombs started to rain
fire over the presidential palace
and President Allende thought
of leaving his body behind
instead of waiting for certain death.

For them
Allende's
suicide is a failure to act.
They may even associate it to destiny and context,

read it as a symbol,
or a mark
of destiny becoming manifest
present in the body of
a man acting as an animal.
As if President Allende in his burning palace
were
a sacrificial lamb.
The proverbial scapegoat.
Even a burrow.
Or the price others have to pay
for Vucub Caquix to keep his burrow safe.

Monumental historians
are really theologians.
And bad ones at that.
For they proclaim the eternal duration of an instant.
They explain events
in terms of the purpose they serve.
And confuse context
with a question of laws of progress
or forces of design,
even though they themselves
no longer believe in such things,
because we no longer can.

Not in the same way as the people of Liège.

III

Those who view reality the as if way,
the monumental way,
declare:
If only we could call out

the evil women and men
who dream of rupture and revolution,
bring them to the dock
of history as tribunal,
kill them before they act,
or measure & calculate,
with the help of clever machines,
the moment of their act,
pre-empt their position,
ponder with forensic precision,
the relative force of the antagonism
engendered by attempts
to bring about historical novelty.

As if
this mediation was the only true representation
As if
negotiation did not require taking
the position
of the other,
to see oneself
through the enemy's eyes,
no
Here, I am here.

Then, at last, they say,
the inquisitor theologians,
the judges of history,
the builders of monuments
& monumental(l) utopias,
then all will be well.
The world or the republic will be pacified,
and utopia will be upheld
at last.

The utopia of order, that is.

One without memorials, only monuments.

Such is the utopia of the Grand Inquisitor,
Vucub Caquix.

IV

Hence, the pact made
between the girl and the jinn.

Hu said to the wind
hopeful that an echo of her words would reach the jinn
We fail to see
really see
the ineradicable nature of that constant,
the erosion of the present that no one can resist,
but which endows life
and the attachment you and I make in it
here and now
with all of their value.
Better to leave,
than seating still
and wait for death.
That is freedom.
And love.
We move, we struggle to be free, we love
because, and only because,
we can lose.

Dream

I

She moved.
Hu moved,
backwards and downwards,
quickly passing a steep
               stair
rivers and barrancas
sailing across
ascending the
               stare
between the eyelid
and the centre of the eye
of Firebird,
passing those they call mojay.

Beyond,
a river of blood
a river of fire.

Hu
got out
and down.

She came upon a crossroads.

The Black One.
The Red One.
The Green One.
The White One.

Crow
went down each road.

In the first he found nothing
In the second he found nothing
In the third he found nothing
In the fourth he found a dream.

A dream of whirlwind,
two lovers,
and the underworld

In the dream
the heavens roared,
the earth shook,
the mouth of hell opened.
There stood a man-bird,
leading the way
to the house from which
none who enters returns.

There's a place there, he said,
where people seat in the dark
eating dust and ash.

There's a place there, he said,
for the great kings of the earth.
Their crowns put away,
they are now slaves
in the house of dust.

There's a place there,
and he pointed to it with his finger bone.
There,

seated on a throne
was the Khan of the Dead
and squatting beneath her feet
the recorder of deeds
keeper of the Book of the Dead.

"Who has brought this one here?"
The Khan said
looking down at Hu
from her throne
in the bowels of the earth.

II

A youngling, a jinn
made of matter so subtle
subtler still than the wind
wakes up in the bottom of a jar.

His heart pounding.
He was she.
Now was he.
Boygirl thought of the one who had cut the chains,
thereby releasing him
from servitude to the witch,
as his lover and sister.
He thought of Hu.
He thought of the moment when the inquisitors captured
in the river of time
a mirror-soul in transit.
He thought of their encounter at sea,
and of the pact they made to struggle so they could be free.

Rather than being sent back to the burrow

they would leave,
leave their body,
imagine a different one,
instead of waiting for death.

Back then
He was she.
Now was he.

Back then,
it had taken ten agonising days for her to die
trapped inside a jar.
Inconsolable,
for she had promised
to meet her sister again
somewhere in Spain.

She wept,
and as she passed away
she left her body behind
to become a boy
and send word to Hu girl
to come rescue him.

III

Crow came back with a dream,
and a message within the dream:

Your sister
no longer her
calls for you
to join him
in the land of the dead.

Here

    Who brought this one here?
asked the Khan at the gates of Hell looking down on me.
I decided to leave my body instead of waiting for death, I said.
The Khan took pity on me, came down and began to show
me everything that men have experienced. Sorrow and wealth.
Happiness and greed. Fortune and misfortune. What would
you take? I'll take stories with me. On one condition, said
the Khan at the gates of the Land of the Dead. That you give
Crow your eyes so you may listen, get others to listen and as
they listen dance to the beat, the bass, the night, for poetry is
music not light. Here. You shall be the first storyteller.

Episode 2. Down In a Hole

Blindness

In all the stories
characters of great wisdom
are often blind.

Or the storytellers themselves
are blind.

It is said that Tarvaa,
the first storyteller,
was blind.

It is said Homer was blind.

It is said that nearing the end of his life,
the Great Homer of the Caribbean
lost his mind,
it went dark,
and in darkness he read the stories of an unknown writer.
Listening to them for the first time
he danced to their music for the first time.

What is the meaning of blindness?
What does it tell us?

Some say it tells us
that stories are a way of seeing,
seeing without eyes.

Others say it tells us
that stories are not about seeing,
that poetry is not made of light,

but music.
A bass-soaked relay
that comes
sometimes in parts,
sometimes in waves
to those who can no longer see or wait.
For stories themselves
come from the darkness.
They're gifts from the dead.

Anti-epic of Gilgamesh

I

Here. I am here.
In the remotest mansions
to find and awaken my brother sister,
duende,
grope after it
in blindness,
wrestle with it
in darkness,
draw near it,
climb together
to places where mountains fuse together into a yearning
of sound
superior to their visible manifestation.

Here I hear the earth shaking.
Trembling as two peaks stretch all the way to heaven
and their bases fall far below the surface.
Here seats Utnapishtim,
the raw poet,
listening with careful attention
to a runaway resonance dilation
that extends from the great flood of old
to the quantum suspension
in the garden of the sun.
Where he was given the gift of life
everlasting,
but only
for as long

as he kept listening.

Here I asked Utnapishtim:
what does he listen to?

Perhaps it's the music of Coyote,
shape-shifting
into a spider,
into
Archie Shepp
doing a saxophone solo
featuring
Raw Poetic &
Damu the Fudgemonk.

The composition slides away from the proposed,
a declining clinamen.
It comes back
a shocking wave
to cultivate another voice
a voice that is alter

        other

than that proposed by one's intention,
angular,
oblique,
the obliquity of unbound reference.[3]

And therefore free.

---

[3] Nathaniel Mackey, *Paracritical Hinge* (Iowa City: Iowa University Press, 2018) 187.

Sound of the outside,
that everlasting outside
in which poets, storytellers, and musicians
enter into a concert
with the outside players
to learn the secret
of how to transition
between genres,
how
to become particle or wave
that reverb saturate
the horizon line of infinite space
and cause a delay
for those who can no longer wait.

In it
the sons and daughters of
all experience
all suffering
all pause
all death
can re
evaluate
and represent
all mysteries…

as they transit from
camel or donkey
to lion
back to child,
and in childhood,
imagine or hear
all mysteries as sound
migrating into the profane

without reservation or nostalgia
all the things that in the dark can be found
as I found them.
As sounds.
For a poem isn't light
but sound
sliding away from the proposed bounds.

If you and I listen to those sounds
and let understanding stop
at what cannot be understood
where the dark folds
into the next second
and the next one
that's where the things of the dark can be found:
the sound of the spirit
its velocity
not the speed of sound
but its interval.

Therein lies
the hesitant possibility of a future,
history as pause.
It slides away from the proposed
it gets into
it comes back
a shocking wave
shape shifting
into the cultivation of another voice
speaking more than one knew what.

This wooing of another voice
entering language and time
in such a way

that I
trans
move
a particle or wave
that reverb saturate
the horizon line of space
and causes a delay

The same darkness delay
that Gilgamesh
entered into
after crossing the gates of hell.

It became thick around him,
thicker still
for there was no light
nothing ahead of him
nothing behind him
but a beat
and at the end of it
another beat
silence interrupted
by the beat of steps
and steps of beat
climin up the mountain,
chill**un,**
didn't come here to stay
if I'm ever gonna see you again
[Brother Sister]
It'll be on judgment day.[4]

---

[4] Le Roi Jones, "Lines to García Lorca," *New Negro Poets: USA*, ed. by Langston Hughes (Bloomington, Indiana: Indiana University Press, 1964) 55.

II

Like Gilgamesh
I didn't come here to stay.
Like him
I came here to listen,
learn to listen
to the man who did not drown.

Learning to breathe.

Only he's now Archie Shepp
finishing his sax solo in
Learning to Breathe

He reaches for another breath
of air.
And the next one.
Raw Poetic picks up the mic

in the air

there is total silence,
until a tiny man,
one of those dancing manikins,
sarcastically murmurs into his ears
for him to repeat:

Beware the illusion of the timeless,
Fill your belly with good things…
dance and be merry,
feast and rejoice,
let your clothes be fresh,

bathe yourself in the music,
cherish the girl
that holds your hand,
and make her happy in your embrace
for this too is the lot of man.[5]

dance
dance again
take one step
and the next one

Here we care nothing about
        ability,
        technique, or
        skill.
Here we are after something else.[6]

Duende.

All that has dark sounds,
has duende.

III

Everything ends.
Palaces to do not stand forever.
Monuments crumble

---

[5] For the sources of these verses see 'The Dispute Between a Man and his Ba' and 'Three Harper's Songs [The Song from the Tomb of King Intef', both in *Ancient Egyptian Literature*, ed. M. Lichteim (Oakland: University of California Press, 2019) 207-14 and 244.

[6] Federico García Lorca, *Deep Song and Other Prose* (New York: New Directions, 1980) 45.

to dust,
the voices of kings and heroes stammer
and the long slender stamen
breaks.
All this is testament
to the passage of time.
Everything ends.

Upon hearing such dark sounds
coming from the mouth
of raw poet
Utnapishtim,
Gilgamesh recoiled.

Like me,
he too had travelled far for a secret.
Instead,
unlike me,
he heard truth
and summoned the courage to live it.

There's a thorny plant,
that flowers underwater.
The stamen of which
is said to heal
cure
restore youth.

Said to Gilgamesh the raw poet Utnapishtim.

Gilgamesh went down.
Deep
Deep
Down

Into the pit.
There he found it.
In the beat.
Such things as one can only find in the deep and dark.
Made his way back to the village of his childhood,
dreaming of eternal youth
happiness and joy.
The happiness of stillness.
He stopped by a cool water well,
but deep in the well,
 unseen by Gilgamesh,
there was a serpent.
Of scales so strong
they seem made of stones,
stamens as old
as a testament.
It smelled the sweetness of the flower,
grabbed it from the hands of Gilgamesh
and shed its skin to avoid been caught
at once returning to the deep.

Gilgamesh stammered.
No
No!
The flower was lost forever,
and as it happens to all who live,
he too
       will die
              one day.

 stones
 stamens
 testaments
 and stammers

the voices of heroes and kings
their palaces
they too
      will pass
           one day.

Allow me,
architecture,
to go down this path
made of
sand
timber
ore
neon light
electricity all round
to fret
the store monuments of Man
with a stick.

Stammament

Allow me,
architecture,
to fret stammens with a little stick,[7]

Hu said.

Did you lift
stone above stone
over him?

Did you light
fire upon fire
upon him,
drowned him
and the world,
under an ocean of tears?

What kind of G-d would do such a thing?

To you
men have build
Stone above stone
Fire upon fire
Cathedrals of fire-crested gold
And in that gold
is
my brother's blood.

Let me have him.

---

[7] Pablo Neruda, *Heights of Macchu Picchu*, 57.

Let me have the brother
you buried here!

Ix Reborn

I cannot know
whether I live
or not
trapped as I am
in the bottom of a jar

set me free
leave my previous body behind
rather than wait for death
for
I can hear
punctuated sounds
of speech
the voice of my lost sister
/lover
/brother
a memory
reclaiming time as being
not of monument
or visuality
reclaiming life in words
to replace the image of progress along a straight line
imagined by those who work forces
against clinamen
against my sliding away from the proposed line

their burning of crosses
staggers
my motion and transition
from camel to lion to child
to time,

a new beginning
after staring into the dark

ascending that stare

retell my tale even if when I sing
my voice
stammers
involuntarily pauses as broken
voices
stamens
of time
or memory flowering into
testament
and testimony
to the dead
during the apotheosis of war
in the land of my childhood.

One pauses
flowers and stammers.
The other is unbreakable and made of marble.

Such is the difference
between memorial and monument,
between song or poetry and the hero's novel.

The latter has come to stand for an occlusion of novelty.

The former paves the way to a new beginning.

A telling needing to be continually retold,
it stammers
involuntarily pauses

retold and reheard like myrtle
stamens
of time flowering
in memory
of our resistant dead

Allow me,
architecture
to fret stone stamens
stammaments
monomonuments
staggermoments
marblestonetestaments
and break free,

reborn.

Memory (2)

Memory (is)
one (brief)
play (or)
experience (of)
temporality (that)
slowing (down)
lost (fiery)
spectres (of)
lost lives (can)
salvage (them)

Lost Lives

Here's to
the lost
the withdrawn
the exiled
the not yet known
and the not yet spoken

Here's to
slowing the time
of what has been said already
slowing it with a greater sense
of care
for the missing
to speed up the spirit
into travelling other dimensions
hidden from view
assist in the creation of a
holding environment
for self-transformation
building bridges
between the said and the unsaid

This entails a relation to
memory.
Within the holding environment,
or imaginary domain,
one
also draws into
play
a sense for past
experience…

which may figure a
temporality
of anti-violence, a
slowing
down... by repair... to keep in mind
lost
traces of that which is missing:
spectres of lost lives.[8]

To salvage them.

---

[8]Brandon La Belle, *Acoustic Justice* (New York & London, Bloomsbury) 17.

Ocean of Sound

> *"Once is maybe enough"*
> *David Toop.*

For you I have crossed
An ocean of sound

pushed it in our mouths pushed it
deep inside
all wrapped in ribbons[9]

of robbed dark memories
dubbed in ambient music.

I was inspired
by your breaking
previously tight divisions which seemed
unbreakable
between genres breaking down
which delivered
earthquakes
to my doorstep but then short changed
by my failure to foresee your dead
heart

---

[9] Pictures of You – The Cure.

now crossing mine in dreaded
despair or unlove not listened
to
even though I kept shouting fully formed
inbroken sentences unpacked
in tears making an ocean of sound.

Other Things to Be Found Underground

Darkness
Isolation
Desolation,

a place

Void of life

like a desert or an ocean
                          (of sound)

Loneliness
                     which can be found among a crowd
                     and does not require solitude
                     or aloneness

A hundred years of
                     men behaving like animals
                     animals behaving like men

Queequeg casting runes
Calchas envisioning a plague,
                     blind prophets

Captain Ahab nailing to the mast a Spanish piece of eight
King Agamemnon capturing the women of Apollo's temple,
                     blinded men

These are other things
to be found underground.
They make stories

Fly off the ground.

On the other side,
sister
brother,
lover,
The Garden.

Future Imperfect (Anti-Novel Manifesto)

I

Who are these foreigners coming to our country?
They bring their words and games
to play with our heads,
they show no shame
even though the pictures they bring with them
seem to us unrecognisable,
and cannot be read.

Don't they know
literature begins with letters,
and anything otherwise
is the ruin and relic
of a preliterary past?

Like the texts of sound and image
alive in sacred sites,
found throughout the native Americas.
Or the visual memory cues of pictographic inscription,
and the lights of Andean khipu,
that show Don Misael and his people ways of voyage
across the abyss of dereliction
left by the paramilitaries when they destroyed his lineage
and imposed the Grand Inquisitor's vision.

Didn't these immigrants see the news? Didn't they die in the crossing?
Go tell them we, the lords of this land,
The Grand Inquisitor
of the Lords of Xibalbá,

call on them to perform
according to our conventions
And the word of our Lords
in the theatres of Laws.
Tell them
in seven days
we shall send our
Home Office team
to play against the foreign twins a game we call 'The Harrowing'.

It is a simple game,
a forensic game,
an interrogation game.
Its final aim:
acceptance of the outcome
as their fate, final place, and name.

II

Seven days later,
the twins
Hu and Ix
came before the officers
in the Home Office's dark house.

Here is your sentence, said the officers.
You can read it,
realise your lives are over,
your fate inevitable,
and succumb.

And when you leave this office,
you can thank your interrogator,
for branding in your skin

the wisdom of our commandments,
the convention of our creed and manners,
And His Word:

There were two in paradise,
And the choice was offered to them:
joy without freedom, or freedom without joy.
There's no other choice.

The rules of the game are quite simple,
said the officers to the twins Ix and Hu.
Do not speak in pictures,
we will only hear believable stories.
But we cannot believe you.
For we declare your nature Evil.
Sex and Hurricane.

III

Tell stories? Sardonically said a twin. I would if I could
but no longer can.
People no longer dare crossing the threshold
to the underworld,
where stories hail from.
We have lost the elements of poetry and music,
no longer know how to deal with mythic matter,
and only a handful of writerly poets,
in a handful of places,
can summon plebeian courage
to bring about new visions,
experimental objects of sound
or lightning essays.
This world has given up on the world of the Nohor,
damned dream-books and word-cinemas,

obscured their ongoing poetics
(despite their force continuing into this century)
and the life of the word.

Instead,
there are novels.
Perfectly crafted, perfectly marketed
best-selling novels.
Written with a mastery no one denies.
But can the euclidean vision of their linear narrative,
do justice
to our stopgap migrant condition?

Perhaps it can expose a secret or two
in the light of forensic judgment.
That there were two in paradise, and a choice was offered to them:
Joy without Freedom or Freedom without Joy.
And that there's no other choice.

But such is the light of today's industries
of performance.
The churches of currency
which destroy the secret
in the moment of its revelation.
And if exposure destroys the secret,
as shaman Don Miguel says
from ancient Amerindian wisdom,
then how to bring about a revelation that does justice to it?

We say secret and we mean hidden truth,
and when you equate secret and truth like this
"it seems to me there's more than a hint

of mystery and fate working in cahoots."[10]

Consider theatre,
dialectics & dialogue,
first figured in the living language
of a poetry to be declared aloud,
the way one declares love,
dramatises an oath,
or declares it broken.
The way young Achilles swore to protect dark-eyed Chalcas,
bearer of doom prophecy.

Dialogue was relocated –
from theatre's stage
to the stage of the reader's mind.
Giving absolute reign to
the adult's imagination of
the child's imagination
which adjudged the latter
to be the fantasy
of children and innocent brutes
condemned to extermination,
thereby burying
the asymmetry of a different past.

We say:
let's bring *critique fantastique* back –
dream-books and word-cinemas,
the vision & world of the Nohor,

---

[10] Michael Taussig, 'The Adult's Imagination of the Child's Imagination' in *Aesthetic Subjects,* ed. by P. Matthews & D. McWhirter (Minneapolis: University of Minnesota Press, 2003) 449.

and the asymmetry of the past,
which moderns declared ruins and relics
forcibly displaced onto
a
homogeneous
empty space,
a museum exhibition,
archived in a final resting place,
supposedly to be protected from the perils of the present,
but in fact,
burned or banned when daring to imagine futures otherwise.

Imagined an instance of misrule and chaos
by the adult's imagination of the child's imagination,
inquisitors and officers
Forced us to abandon them.
They command
to
bow our heads
to the west where the sun sets
and accept as inevitable fate
that death triumphs
desire is betrayed
no joy without pain
and nothing can be reserved
For the coming days.

Lo, we unfold our darkness
and on this rock place,
this marble-like cold place,
Which is said to be our final resting place,
a new pact we declare.
Laws of peace, of love, of cohabitation ... another way
For when the way is lost,

says the old Book of the Way,
there's alliance not allegiance.
When there's alliance, there's justice.
And with justice, the new rites and ceremonials.
Which are the end of loyalty and allegiance
to the single vision
of the Grand Inquisitor.

In the new pact, the poetries of
critique fantastique & masque
Would no longer be flattened into plot,
nor subjectivity be confused with
authenticity
or identity
or marble-like character.

We refuse to swear allegiance to the symmetry (of plot)
and to collapse all dimensions of literature
into those of
The homogeneity of the group,
inner space
& commerce.

IV

Tell stories? wondered the other twin. I would if I could.
but we K/c/ant.
People no longer dare crossing the threshold to the underworld,
where stories hail from.
We have lost the elements of poetry and music,
no longer know how to deal with mythic
matter,
and only a handful of writerly poets,
in a handful of places,

can summon plebeian courage to bring about new visions,
experimental objects of sound
or lightning essays.

We gave up on the inner life of the word,
gave up on the world of the Nohor,
relinquished our dream-books and word-cinemas.
Instead,
we have novels
perfectly crafted novels
written with a mastery no one denies. We have
televised news & melodramas.

But in these novels,
if a girl speaks to her dead sister
or a boy runs into the forest of ghosts
after the paramilitary set their house on fire,
if that boy or girl ran into
woods
or escaped by sea from dystopia
or fell through a hole underground leaving their body behind
to be preserved at the bottom of the sea
or in those
woods,
for tomorrow's sake,
rather than wait for death,
then they're adjudged
Backward
Or Brute,
And the decree is proclaimed:
Exterminate All the Brutes!

And if in that instant
their sister's lifeless body seeps up to them from beneath

and returns
to subtle matter
(how long is this instant?)
nuzzled in the crook of what once was their father's or
mother's arm
so that,
fist balled against
God
Earth
Sky High,
that boygirl weeps over bodies
in their House of Ice
his
her
mouth
agape behind a hurricane
unable to react
mute
not willing to compute
or relate the facts,
then that is judged not to be true
it isn't realism
couldn't count as hi-fidelity literature
nor be registered
as what may be considered believable.

Today's industry of performance
advises that the page or the camera be all-seeing.
The audience wants to see it all.
Not to struggle for liberation.
But only to matter.
All that matters, all that,
especially mattering.

All Lives Matter.

This is the panopticon of voyeurism.

To be realistic & believable,
today's industry of performance says:
set aside,
onto a backwards space & time,
the other things that might not pass the test of the forensic eye
of the praetorian class
(a flick of the hand
a gesture of wonder or surprise
a fleeting glance at the lens,
and the take is rubbish).

V

The revolution will not be televised,
But our protest will be sampled.
A bass-soaked overlay
That reverb saturates
Black matter
Opening
To liberate
La frontera border en el fin.
A void vortex,
An open wound.
In the ironic gesture
Of native storier Charles Aubid
When he waived back his raised hand
To Judge Lord
Of the High Court
And refused allegiance

To those who had commanded to His People:
One King, One God, One Law.

VI

Consider Charles Aubid,
Native Storier
of the White Earth Reservation.

Many moons ago
no one knows how many
Charles Aubid,
wordsmith of the Chippewa nation,
declared by stories the preservation
Not the authenticity of his nation
but their survivance in native presence.

Before a Federal Court
in an autumn moon
more than
no one knows
how many
many moons ago,
Charles Aubid raised his hand.

He
listened to the Christian oath,
broken many times,
no one knows
how many,
many moons ago.
An oath
spoken
for the first time

in the language of the Anishinaabe
invented by Crow and Coyote in the time before time.

Charles Aubid waved back his raised hand
at US District Judge Miles Lord,
an ironic take on that oath,
and spoke of natural reason & continental freedom
figured more than
no one knows
how many
many moons ago
when Coyote and Crow
came together and for the first time
told stories
weaving together sound and thought.

Charles Aubid told stories
that afternoon
In the Court of Judge Lord.
From memory,
which he shared,
he said,
with all matter
shattered
by the manifest violence of the colonisers.
Hailing all that matters,
not just All Lives,
but Liberation & The Tree of Continental Freedom,
Charles Aubid opened for the judge his stories.

In his stories
a further person
figured from visual memory comes to presence.
Old John Squirrel,

a visual reminiscence
of when the elder spoke
of the right to wild rice harvest,
manoomin
they called it,
practised many moons ago
no one knows
how many
on the shores of Rice Lake in Minnesota.

As it was agreed with the officers of the US government
no one knows
how many
many moons ago
on the same shores.

Charles Aubid said he was there,
When Old John Squirrel
met with the Federal agents.
When Old John Squirrel
submitted to their harrowing
interrogations
When Old John Squirrel
responded from memory to their claims for evidence.
And he listened carefully
When Old John Squirrel
was told by the inquisition officers
that the White Earth Nation would always keep its rights
to harvest wild rice.

Charles Aubid told
All who listened
That afternoon
In the Court of Judge Lord

that the Anishinaabe always invoked their rights
by stories.

But they did not listen.

He told Judge Lord
that Old John Squirrel was there
in those stories
and by those same stories he was made present that day in
court.

But Judge Lord did not listen.
Not because he did not know.
But because he did not want to know.
Such is the Art of Mastery.

John Squirrel is dead,
Judge Lord said,
looking down on the Anishinaabe wordsmith Charles Aubid
from his judge's chair,
and you cannot say what a dead man said.

The Lord of the Court
Judge Miles Lord
could have heard
Aubid's testimony.
And listened
to that testimony,
in that testimony
the visual trace
and memory
of an agreement
spoken
many moons ago

no one knows
how many.

But what he heard that day in court was hearsay,
and therefore unbelievable,
Judge Lord said.

Instead of learning
and listening,
Instead of learning
to listen,
Judge Lord
sided with the Federal Attorney,
A Bureaucrat of the Burrow,
who had objected
that in accordance with the forensic precision
of inquisitorial procedure
only the law's provision
of equal (white) masks without presence
can be admitted
to be timeless
unchangeable
believable.

There's no room in the burrow for poetry or stories.

VII

The Harrowing Interrogators
The Burrowing Bureaucrats
Of the Burrow
the
Inquisition Officers
& Policeniaks

of the Home Office
The US Federal Agents
Judge Lord
The Lords of the Dark Place of Xibalbá
and the bird-demon named Vucub Caquix
are more than characters.

They embody The Architecture,
The Framework,
The Manners,
The Spectacle
& Creed
of a society.

They show to us what happens
when that society descends
into a cult of
Architecture,
Framework,
Manners,
Spectacle
& Creed

in which no room is left for poetic memory and stories.

If a novel cannot show us
that hidden reality
If it cannot show us an alternative reality
if it cannot make room for the rhythm of poetic memory
& the music of its landscape
if it sides instead with Judge Lord
& the Lords of the Dark Place
If it remains
deaf

To the stories of Charles Aubid
To the connection between the living and the resistant dead,
and builds
Instead
only monuments on the page,
all the worse for the novel
of this age.

No matter how loudly the novel declares itself
Realist.
No matter how hard it tries to address
the gaze of a disembodied audience,
self-referencing and distant,
each one of them holding
placards over their heads,
with their proper places,
property holdings
& CEO Heads.

If that novel
has nothing to say
about the continuance of the stories
Charles Aubid told the court
that afternoon,
no one knows how many
many moons ago.
If that novel
has nothing to say
about the appreciation of pre-existing wealth
Justified
As though it were an uninhabited continent
then
at the very least
the novel will have to be reinvented.

It would be best –
best for literature and for society if it stammers,
if the novel
fails
hesitates
giving us time,
time to think
time to time
The time
which is memory & life
which is what the life of the word is.
Living memory not silent monuments.

Stammers are resonances
allowing for time's transit
carrying the long past
on into a future otherwise
than it was.
Transforming that resonance
to make us pause and hesitate
its reverb moving in a wave
to make something happen in us
that can no longer wait.

Aesthetic ideas
they show us the way
principles or new beginnings
with the force to carry
The long past
on into and create
a future otherwise.

If they show the way to utopia,
it is not utopia as it is supposed to look like.

Certainly not the Grand Inquisitor's utopia.

If the word
[utopia]
is to be redeemed,
it will have to be
by someone that cannot be redeemed.

Someone like
Hu and Ix
who followed utopia into the abyss
[which yawns behind the Grand Inquisitor's vision
like the open jaws of the jaguar behind the King
in the painting by El Greco]
and clambered on
to the other side with their symbols and tricks.

The symbol which Trickster
embodies and keeps
within
is not a static one
not an unchanging one
not an authentic one.

There's no such thing,
only transformation
& motion.

If so,
let understanding stop at what cannot be understood.

That would be the highest achievement.

Wilson Harris

Consider Wilson Harris,
surveyor of the inner territory of Guiana
a prolific student
of the indigenous wordsmiths of the territory of Guiana
becoming the wordsmith of the territory of Guiana.

He declared by stories
the survivance & memory of such native presence
showed us
word-cinemas
and dream-spaces
drawn out from a dream-map
of uncanny spaces
in the interior of Guiana.

That is a high achievement,
figured in the eye of the Scarecrow,
appeared
or evoked,
in the head of Crow's relative,
                    Raven.

In The Tree of the Sun
he showed us London seen through other
                              eyescapes
he observed
that the equation of catastrophe with
        a specific hinging moment in time
is a convention
born
many moons ago

no one knows how many
though it can be seen already
in the tale of Oedipus
when the king strikes an old man in a dispute at a

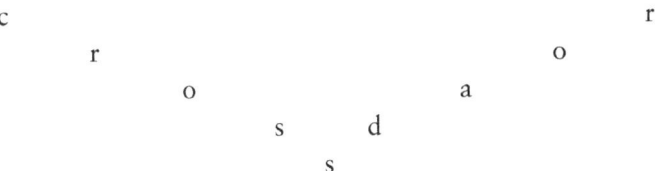

With that action
a prophecy is fulfilled.
The king has entered fate
        unchangeable fate
        inextricable fate
he's now subjected to fate's
praetorian precision
and timeless laws.

Such forensic precision
imagines symmetry
as a pact,
between Oedipus's act and the past,
its effects taking place in such a way
that place itself,
timespace,
is coerced.
It becomes consecutive and flat
and the king's motion in spacetime
a succession of points

rather than events –

final
fixed
fatal.

They can be forever divided
into ever smaller points
and yet there's no way
Oedipus will escape his past
just as there's no way
Achilles will catch up with the tortoise.

Bring your ingenuity toolbox,
measure that divide
calculate its extension
express it in numbers
zero or one.
Logically, as
this or that,
or as a Manichean divide,
them versus us;
measure it
or its performance,
mistake numerical succession
for a temporal pattern or destination
make it calculable
manageable
and ready to hand –
an uninhabited continent
out there for the taking
that someone will occupy.

Now flash forward a few centuries,

into our time of security and pre-emption,
obsessed with calculation
and with putting a prize
on the risk-variations of a flattened time.
Mistaking plot for reality,
teleology for history;
imagine that future
of even cleverer machines
and tighter prohibitions
liminal prohibitions
security repressions
over trans

...and there you have it,
that's the world Hoodoo Girl escaped from in Book 1

The adult's imagination
of the child's imagination.
A flattening of all dimensions
into those of the page
or the plane of representation
together with the Gothic ideal of presentation.

A flattening of all that goes into figuration

including
the flick of a hand   weaving
a gesture of surprise   wonder
a fleeting glance at the lens   worlding
which is what Coyote and Crow did
when they first put together thought and sound
brains
muscles
a hand (raised in ironic gesture at the lord of the ball court)

the expenditure of energy over time,
all that,
is flattened
to fit the dimensions
of page & commerce

just because, in theory,
you could go on cutting spacetime in half
and on and on
voyeuristically zooming in
forever and ever
on smaller and smaller
units of sliced time.

But when you try to frame reality
into the unchanging yardstick of judgment,
to grasp our everyday experience in spacetime,
to visualise those unchanging solids,
you will engender Euclidean utopias
that no one can touch
but can crush real lives.
In that way
we engender the very strangeness
that the blind Argentinian prophet noted,
time and again,
as he went down a basement in a flat
in Buenos Aires
a thousand years after the patron saint
of dialogue and dialectic.

The problem is
neither
dialogue nor dialectic
but the mistake

of trying to measure transformation and motion
in an object
or event
as it is in itself.

A mistake
which is common
to forensic novels
and monumental history
when turned into a convention
it is used as a yardstick
according to which
crisis or catastrophe
should be understood
as a hinging moment in time.

A moment
that can be grasped or precisely described.
Call it fate
or context,
that convention, that yardstick,
the symmetry of space and time,
leaves no space for asymmetry -
the past
the weird -
memory,
or the fantastic magic of a dispute at a crossroads.

And no room for stories or poetry.

That is the utopia of the Inquisitor,
Vucub Caquix
and the Lords of Xibalbá.

Episode 3. Standoff

The Trial

On our day in court
The Lords of Xibalbá
decided to subject us
to three further trials.

The House of Videodrome
The House of Knives
The House of Ice.

In them
many things could be found.

A desert
a vast ocean
the island of the Minoans with its labyrinth
                and the monster at its centre
Scorpion Men
A beast on the outside, a man underneath
or the very opposite
Jekyll and Hyde
roaming the streets of Edinburgh.

La isla de las muñecas en México
Dr. Moreau's island,
or the one in which Dr. Morel's machine
can capture a fugitive's soul
in a mirror soul
and project it
day after day
until it becomes reality
for the visitors of the island.

Hades,
Argentina under the military junta
or the neo-fascists who call themselves
libertarian.

The domed boroughs of ExLondon
after a century and a half
of neoliberal doom.

The land of the Khan
that Gilgamesh visited.

A vast digital ocean of sound
the bush of ghosts
the Pequod
La Jeté
the past present and future of Ebenezer Scrooge
the land of the Vikings
laid to waste in Ragnarok's wake.

The Morlocks' cave
the palace of Siddhartha
Dresden or Hiroshima
Bogotá ca. 1991
Xibalbá
País de la penumbra.

Videodrome (Found Poetry)

Forget Game of Thrones.
Time to kill off the elves and get weird,
I read on a post online.

Aren't we bored
to death
of the European mediaeval settings of
fantasy tv series
and videogames?

What about rpg games
set in a post-colonial world
where all surviving peoples
tremble and transform
into coyotes and crows
at the merest sight
of the tyranny that enslaved them?

No more Baldur's Gate 3.

Forget Game of Thrones.

Here's to Geralt de Rivia
drowning in his own shit

                            (acting)

Why not weirder places like
El país de la penumbra
or weirder characters like Huhnapú
            (the character formerly known as Hoodoo Girl)
and Ixbalanqué

(transiting from sister to brother)
who become lovers
while venturing down in a hole
to find underground
the elements of story
and save the world from drowning?

Now, that would be something
Worth playing.

I'm sick 'n tired
of our tolerance for Eurovision-inspired
folklore,
and fucking Tolkien,
who,
while tattooed on my back
has entirely run out.

I get it.
We're beholden to this fucking
neon bitch
you-got-me-from-behind existing universe.

But let's be frank.
The world of Toril,
where the Forgotten Realms are located,
is one of the most boring places
of the entire D&D universe.

Especially when compared
to the wonderful dissonance & mess
of the planes of the void
between worlds
which make me wanna guess

if in the next Spelljammer campaigns
victory or success
could be measured less
by the number of magical beings
and spells,
and more,
by the quality of mindflayers,
bodyhorror,
and druids having sex
with clerics.

Who look like the Lords of Xibalbá
trying to destroy
me and my twin lover
sisterbrother.

And don't get me going
on the fucking multiverse.
It is a hypothetical collection
of potentially diverse
observable universes.
Did you not hear hypothetical?

As for comic books,
give me Batman's cave any day.

House of Knives
(Found Poetry)

I can't remember shit
past 10:30

What I don't know won't hurt me,
especially if I know how not to know it.

Give me a pack of 'rillos and a scratch-off lottery.
Here.
Life of the fucking party, eh?
Drunk as fuck.
You lose always, said the blind prophet.
There's always one of those in these stories.
Always one like this.
Yeah. That's it.
The chemistry of the chemistry means
I can't remember shit
past 10:30

I don't do that usually,
getting drunk as fuck,
I mean,
not
usually
deadely

But they're off cocaine 'n ketamine here
at the gates of Hell or the Glen in LA.

I rather smoke
a little weed and wait no more

for the fucking hero to appear.
I don't do that usually, deadly,
but in this place
they're off cocaine and ketamine
and I keep drowning in the asphalt
as I walk to the shop in The Glen in LA.
Or is it hell?

While I wait no more
for the hero to appear
I'll crack the goddamn door wide open
let the fire go
and mama is no longer.

Only an empty room
but I couldn't help crying
told my little sister you remind me of someone else,
y'know that,
and got on
escaped
got on with the tv show.
I ain't never had no little sisterbrother.
I still love him though.
Found him,
y'know?
We're on a quest to go back to the insanity.

House of Ice

In the House of Cold & Ice

(a wagon in the Train of Fire and Ice,
which Manu and his crew took from
Santa Marta and Bogotá)

my lover sisterbrother and I
faced ice
                              for the first time
and a death squad
                              for the second time
as we made our way
up north
having crossed the Rio Bravo

(read Stix)

from the south.

How's this, they aren't dead yet?
Asked the Lords of Xibalbá
To their border militias and home office bitches.

Then set the jaguars free,
to bring us to Ntu,
the point from which creation begins.

But before their predator's teeth
sliced us 'n diced us
we made them dance
'til we turned the house on fire.

This is now the house of blues 'n fire.

Here, first is the salad
then the meat
then the vegetables…
WAIT,
we said,
quoting Oliver Lake,
bring all our food at one time
and on the same plate,
bring
Dixieland
Be-bop
Soul
Rhythm 'n blues
Cool school
Swing & avant garde
Free jazz
Rock
Jazz rock
Drill and Grime

WHAT KIND OF MUSIC DO YOU PLAY?
they asked,
THE GOOD KIND,
we replied,
fooling once again
the Hound of the Underground
the migra and the repo men
with their jaguar teeth.
The bats,
and the vampire bat,
the one they call Camazotz,
which sucks the life out of all mankind

disguised as a Wall Street
suit 'n tie.

When they went to war
in the lands of our childhood
we got to hide ourselves
in the clubs underground.

In Barbarie &
The Backrooms.

To survive the apotheosis
of capital & war
in the lands of our childhood.

We were children back then,
spoke and did as children do,
hid ourselves
in our music & dance
to survive.

But now I'm all grown up,
so I showed my head
through the door
the day before
and the day after
we partied all night.

And it was cut at once
by the regime,
Camazotz,
the vampire bat,
disguised as ESMAD riot police
and the good people of Cali.

Are you awake? Is it morning yet?
You're all silent, Hu,
you don't hop,
slide or jump to their every command.
Which is all well and good,
but why did they call to the house
at this godforsaken hour
and not in normal office ones during the day, tell me that.
Listen to me love,
they'll ring back tomorrow
or the day after tomorrow
or the one after that,
and they'll say
we don't know what happened,
it was many moons ago how many no one knows.

Hu's body remains silent
as if standing before Ix
though his eyes have turned to the tv,
mute, couldn't answer.

I would have liked to say it's nine 'o clock,
it's ok,
but I couldn't 'cause I had lost my head.

We've been defeated and vanquished, Ix said.

He called all the animals,
all the performers
and all the dancers.

Aretha Franklin & Sun Ra
Coltrane & The Dixie Hummin Birds
Miles & Muddy Waters, same.

Depeche Mode
soda & the cure, same
... for there's no, i can't get no, no,
LABELS DIVIDE! SEPARATE
my head
but the sounds make it whole again,
not to separate the oral from the literary.
One music – diff feelings & experiences but same,
the total sound-mass sound-
hear (here) all the players as one.[11]

---

[11] Sources, cut-ins and samples from online music posts, liner notes and, principally, from Oliver Lake, "Separation", in *Ntu: Point From Which Creation Begins* (Arsita/freedom, 1976).

and all the birds sing bass

Guilléncollage

"

Quieren que estemos Muertos[12]
para adornar la casa del Gran Jefe
pero
los grandes MUERTOS... no mueren nunca.
No porque hayas caído
Tu LUZ será menos alta
Y no porque te QUEMEN
En calle y plaza, contra el PUÑAL, PECHO y coraza
hablar[emos] indiferentes
del SOL,
de la Lluvia,
o la tormenta
que nos desplaza.
Te entrego mi poema, algarabía
en lengua de piratas
donde todo el material habla
creaking the word algarabía
back to moorish Spain
with Federico García Lorca
noisy chatter between trabajar
duende
and Cuba
Federico,
Granada,
y Primavera.

Or improv jazz

---

[12] For the source of the verses sampled here, Nicolas Guillén, *Antología de la poesía cósmica de Nicolas Guillén* (Méjico: Frente de Afirmación Hispanista, 2001) 9, 22, 26, 33 and 49.

& hip hop
featuring Archie, Raw Poetic & Damu the Fudgemunk
creaking the improv into deep song
trip hop
carretón
of broken phrases
in prose-poetic manifesto letters
reaggaetón
drawn from mythlandscapes
& the liner notes of album presses
sampling or juggling different genres
moving maps, searching soles, or masked hidden faces
among the people policed into tight racial spaces.

Poetic Music Laundry List

Professor Shepp, Raw Poetic
You and I
A Love Supreme
The Nova Ghost Set   (AND)
Deconstructive Woodwind Chorus
The East Bay Dread Ensemble
The Mystic Horn Society
Molimo m'Atet
Sex Bob-Omb
Jossie and the Pussycats
Barry Jive & the Uptown Five
aka Sonic Death Monkey
aka Kathleen Turner Overdrive
Las Kellys The Kelly Affair The Carrie Nations
Fuck
The Archies
BUT
God Save
The Unrepentant Gays
Hedwig and The Angry Inch
Otis Day and the Knights
(Oh, how I loved them.
It was dark in the cinema that day,
and I kissed you)
Ellen Aim and The Attackers
CBGBsCB4
Eddie and The Cruisers
Figrin D'an and the Moodal Nodes
Stillwater
Citizen Dick
Slavoj & The Masterbators

Jazz Sabbath
(Here come)
The Lords of the Underworld

To leave your body before death arrives
and walk towards the Sun from the dark,
listen to & recite the previous incantation,
while gyrating on a turntable.

Charon

Dear friend across the river
come 'n take us away from here,
away from this hellish red,
dad
come back 'n
carry us away from here,
my sister and I
woke up from the war
to the sound and noise
of the silence that allows
the chatter of my voice
to become a shockwave in return
washing away the pain.

Turn around
put my ear down to the ground
and hear the stories being told
we've been searching to behold
the elements underground
with which stories will be told
> again
> at war's end
> when we'll be bold

enough
to ask for whom the bell has tolled.

My back now to the world
to the inquisitor's world
the night of the world
to the witch who was smiling when my mother died,
who

took my mirror and soul,
but they say
once you turn
they'll try to kill us
        break us   hate us
so we'll never be saints
brother sister
only enemies.

My beautiful
Ix-
you and I
are ready
to make our next move
dance better
even if they kill us
break us
hate us
for here we are
listening to the freakwaves
protopoppunks
and skaindls
sldniaks

gyrating on a turntable
getting' caught stealin'
a little blue ball,
the fire of sound,
chased by policeniaks
                who want to jail us into racial
                          spaces.

                          We won't let them,
we'll dance-fight

until you or I get our heads bashed up.
But don't worry.
I will move to the side,
and you shall get a pass.

I've seen your face here
under the tables
underground
you can tell me your fears and fantasies
what brings you
round
here
to the lost & found
down underground

down underground
we found,
you and I,
we found
the Hounds of the Underground.
Two children fleeing
the war-torn lands of our childhood
to end up fleeing
war-torn ExLondon.

Sit. Down.

down underground
with the hounds
in the undercity
we're growing up and gettin' out
lookin' to write our own stories,
even if the song remains the same,
the same ol' story

of topside and bottomdown
down
down underground.

We swore never to betray each other,
our people,
but fight for them,
o tell me,
don't you recall
when we painted on that wall
a giant middle finger,
and promised each other
to keep our little secrets.

One day this city will respect us,
'cause we found
in exLondon bedlam
the backrooms and back corridors
through which every boudoir in Clapham
became a light beam,
whisking us away,
as if by sorcerer's magick,
to other games
in other planets
not this one.

I woke up to the sounds.
They kill us break us hate us.
We were just girls back then
You and I
You're now my lover
sister
brother

and I
an enemy of the state
'cause I've dwelled in the arcane
mirror-souls
books
darkspells
and sounds

be-bebop
free jazz
drill and grime
punk and funk
with Archie, Raw Poetic & Damu the Fudgemunk

weird videogames
post-futurity child toys
but
as the blind prophet said
that post
might turn out
to have been
premature
 after all.

She Raves Tragedy

She raves a tragedy
        she might
        or might not like it
but once she takes to the stage
she contains
only half   of it
once she takes up the fight
she unleashes
the other half
herself all ears and eyeballs
exploding atoms, rays, and fire
leaping and lifting her
above
across the space
they just passed
she defeats the Moirai
just like fire would
but
the ground has no open mouth
but
it swallows any and all
Fates or fate
and the girl
she looks beautiful
in her spotted sun o' the night
jaguar ensemble
once she takes to the stage
and sets it on fire.

Jaguar and leopard
her tail in the leotard

she sure looks good
ascending from the cave to the stage
from Antigone to Sailor Moon
too chic to leap but ready to strike
she knows true tragedy
like love
is atmospheric
gravitational
it surrounds us
slices us
claws are laws
tear us apart
                revealing
what she hides
behind the silks and sequins of
Spain
Adrian
or Bob Mackie

She raves a simulation of tragedy
an imitation of life
                and as such
                she is true to life
                truer than most
since nothing is authentic
unmasked or not theatrical,
at least in the sense that there is no outside
to the totality of things,
when a Black woman speaks,
only internal perspectives
which are partial
and reflect one another
as the facets of one of her diamonds

no fate here
no vision of an ultimate judgment
or the perfect coincidence
between knowledge and being
yielding to calculation
an unknowable path

and there's the tragedy
                          her tragedy
                          our tragedy
like the cosmos repeating itself
after an unimaginable time
but there's no Angel of History
to notice it
no justice
just us

true tragedy
is atmospheric and
gravitational
(she)
goes back to the cave
to find in the dark
the elements of story
that
when put together
bring
memory
back
and behind it
time

(she)
shows us that to tell anything, to register it

she must take a small step to the side
make present her subtle difference
from it
so that being and knowledge never fully coincide

tale & tragedy are atmospheric and
gravitational
in that regard
they
can only happen
when she takes to the stage
when she takes up the fight
a black woman speaks
she sings
she stands
afloat, goes up, comes back to the light
she speaks
she sings
she stands
at the abarian point between field forces
burning in her path those who burn crosses
afloat
up
and light

like Greta Garbo
Tippi Hedren
David Bowie

or Judy Garland
telling the Great and Powerful

                                        (Oz)

he can fuck

                                               off

O dear Judy.
Her death
in time
before time
on 22 June, 1969
was the spark
that ignited the night
of New York on 3 July
when firestarters of all kinds
set the city ablaze
a rave for the times

she did
like I did
just like fire would do
set alight
our council state flat
on 3 June, 2069
burning the inquisitors and the police
    for shutting down Bowie
    and Judy Garland
    whose death sparked a fire
    that burns
    from Stonewall to Popham State
    bringing Suella & The Liar
    to their final fate

She speaks
She is black, mayan,
'n slave
so we don't have to

las bolleras
las galas

las trans
las marías
las latinas en drag
Hu y Antígona
Sophia, Zoe y Nayra
You

a Black woman speaks
she sings
she stands

                she shows us no goddess
                will come down
                to save us

Rita Hayworth
Liz Taylor
Frida Kahlo
Ramona
Lady Gaga

They rave justice
Speak sing 'n dance
doing justice
raving vengeance
because justice
is never ours

She raves revenge
                        on the lords of this dark land
while we plot on it
on sleepless
nights

their revolt
may be domesticated by the market
a failed revolution
a vicarious triumph

But it don't matter.

We don't need a goddess.
She doesn't need us either.

Call and Response

On the phone
after listening to her tape
the police officers asked her name

I gave them only the middle
finger

"Music"
a mask made of wind, of wrack
by which if
by wind it meant soul it meant
salvage[13]

not savage

a certain wariness of culture
masks
and identity masks
and performance

music
subjected to subjunctive relay work of qualm
verging on evacuating the light & sound
masquerade
(performance also, then, in that sense)
that music is, the graphic and acoustic masquerade

---

[13]Nathaniel Mackey, *Whatsaid Serif* (San Francisco: City Lights, 1998) 21.

that poetry is[14]

possessed or problematic speech
the thing found in the dark

call and

---

[14]Nathaniel Mackey, *Paracritical Hinge* (Iowa City: University of Iowa Press, 2018) 233.

Call and _____ (2)

There is something in common
                                        between

poetry
love
an atom
García Lorca's cante jondo
and Blck music
    a
a rapidly vibrating guitar string
making waves
lifting her up
out of the cave

And as it happens
                                        with

poetry
love
an atom
García Lorca's cante jondo
and Blck music
    a
when she speaks
she sings
she   takes up the fight
        takes to the stage
in the waves
you can never see the _____ itself.

Centrifugal Poem

It begins with an ironic wave to the lord of the court
it bids all givens goodbye
it bides time for what words will not do
                      what perspective will not do
                      what the novel will not do
                      what the joy of work
        and the consolations of philosophy will not do

The joy of work and the consolations of philosophy
accrue their primitive accumulation value
to a horizon it wants to get across and beyond,
abandoning the joy of work, the mastery of the novel,
and the consolations of philosophy,
or seeking new ones.

It will, of course, be marginalised
especially when listened to
on the phone on tape or on a digital file
sent from the   island   of Papayal
by the wordsmith of Las Pavas
or spoken by a Blck girl coming back
from the bowels of the earth

Blck centrifugal writing and indigenous alternate voices
have been
continue to be
multiply marginalised
sent back to relic time
unremittingly
but why would it be otherwise?

At a time when...
critical discourse battens on identity obsession
centrifugal writing reorients identity
in ways that defy prevailing divisions of labour.
In the face of widespread fetishisation of collectivity,
it dislocates collectivity,
flies from collectivity,
wants to make flight a condition of collectivity.[15]

It lets go of the Angel of History in favour of the Ghost of Chance.
This is one of the lessons it
(critique)
has learned from Blck music.

It is, like any other art, not new but imaginative,
 inventive,
productive
and/our outside.

To the extent that it addresses the wings of
and dresses in the wings of
all resistances
indigenous to its practice and medium,
ranging from the amorous touch of love
to the agonistic embrace of deep sound
the fission of an atom
the rapid vibration of a string or a drum skin

sending its fire
in all directions

---

[15] Nathaniel Mackey, "Destination Out" in *Paracritical Hinge*, 239 for quote and the source of this poem.

in waves
but in them you cannot see the _____s.

Demonic rub,
it speaks in alternate voices,
recorded
on a tape
a digital file
on the phone
time
and again.

Something unknown
doing
we don't know what
which is the total sum
of the joys of our work
and the consolations of our philosophy.

Do not wear them,
Wings,
as if they were the stuff
and essence of our community
but only eight slithy toves gimbaling and gyrating
on a turntable
in the oxygen wave,
particle and wave,
the
remains of the subtle fire wave that made
Ix the jinn and Hu girl
together like lovers in a whirlwind

in demonic embrace.

The centrifugal poet is not nearly so concerned
with describing the facts
as with creating light & sound
image-systems
that make something happen in us
which lift us up
and bring us dancing back down
to the brief history of this instant.

Lords Doubt

After listening on the phone on the tape

her voice
digitally altered
on a Teenage Engineering PO
sounding like the centrifugal destination
of a post-expectant futurity

the Lords of Xibalbá
asked the blind prophet
and his deaf companion

Why haven't we vanquished the twin lovers?

That was their moment of fall and ruin.
But
wait
there's a history to every instant
no matter how brief
and this one is no exception.

Hu and Ix
had already spoken
to Xulú, the blind prophet
and Pacam, his deaf companion.

We've felt a promise, premise, and premonition,
they told them.

That the lords of this dark country
will use firestones and mirrors

to break us kill us hate us
that they're in doubt
thinking what to do
that they're measuring
with precision
the size of this instant
how to seize it,
grab hold of it.

They will ask you how
to break us kill us hate us.

They will say:
break their bones with a chainsaw
put them in a conveyor-belt
throw them in the crusher
make them dust.
Put them in a field and bomb the bastards!

It isn't convenient, you will say to them,
for they will be reborn after the first day

Then they will say:
hang them from the cannibal trees
splinter the names
use them as white paint
to cover the who gave the order graffiti with low-lying spray,
make them invisible, get them lost.

It isn't convenient, you will say to them,
for they will be reborn after the second day.

Then they will say:

take them on a carpet-bombing helicopter ride
push them from up high
make them fall.

It isn't convenient, you will say to them,
for they will be reborn after three days.

Then, exasperated, they will say:
What would you have us do?

And you will say to them:
the lovers,
they're poets aren't they?
They're searching for the elements of story.
Isn't that why they came down underground?
If so,
make them perform.
Performance is a most bothersome and inconvenient word
for writerly poets
like being thrown into a river after being burnt in an oven fire.

Sight-specific prose poem, or not

Performance is a bothersome and inconvenient word for writerly poets, someone said. I agree. Spoken word, poetry slams, lit festivals, and word jams have made the term and what we do tantamount to or even synonymous with the antics of theatricality and spectacle: a recourse to monumentality, to the plight of the hero placed in a hinging moment of catastrophe, the declamatory, persuasive or pleasing rhetoric, and the inner motifs of a scandal. Such tactics have become widespread in the framing of news narratives, in so-called autofiction, and in the novel. They aim at propping up words and sounds or helping them appear more effective, suggestive, or persuasive. It makes sense in times like these, now that every single one of our aspects and innermost intentions can be captured on screen by a smartphone device or a camera. They work pushing forces like the obsidian mirrors of old. And as in the Rage Against the Machine song, those who work to push forces are often the same that burn crosses. Underpinning such attitudes is the assumption that words are inert when left on their own or at least weaker than marble architectures and unchangeable frames. Vegetable-like. The history of that assumption would take us back to colonial times in the Americas. When European chroniclers marvelled at the oratory powers of indigenous wordsmiths, at the same time as they would dismiss such popular practices of fine performance art as relics that attested to the myrtle-like nature of their soul and mind. Which these chroniclers supposed as fluid as the rain and rivers of the forests, and as changing, multitudinous, and excessive in their appetite as the vegetation or the predators of the jungle. And, therefore, weaker in comparison to the strength of the fortress architectures and fortitude virtues of

Christian mores. It may not be a coincidence that the tropes expressing these assumptions, coming from the visualisations of martial architecture, Euclidean geometry, and defensive mentalities became established around the seventeenth century. At the same time as notions of spatial theatre and gothic symbolism engendered and pervaded a culture of political spectacle, expansion, and takeover of space from European centres to the rest of the world. Beginning but not only in the Americas. The tropes, presuppositions, and the basic assumptions informing such attitudes can be seen in the frontispiece of the book *Leviathan*, itself a symbol and trope for the beast of darkness and order-out-of-chaos, published in 1651. That kind of illusionistic representation or theatre must be contrasted with presence and opposed to the perhaps older political potential of presentational image-systems in which landscape, light & sound come together to make present other spaces and time dimensions. In these imaginary domains the past, being past, is brought to bear on the present and the future in a way that can make present, for us, the many variations and possibilities that lie ahead of us. Not because we can know them as a certain path into the future but precisely because we can't. They show us that the future is open. The contrast between presence and theatricality means we can no longer describe in an evaluative way the so-called primitive mind *as if* it lacked the capacity to conceive of a distinction between truth and falsehood, or *as if* it lacked the strength of will to sustain that distinction. We cannot speak of such things *as if* there were a hinging moment when the mind finally develops its powers of abstraction and critical reason becomes ironic. Such "as if" discrimination between "our" newly formed (modern) subjectivity and "their" presumed lack of it is pedantic. And most likely unwarranted, as a growing mountain of archaeological evidence shows. It would be better to see in that contrast the presence in language of varying experiences of spatiality and time. Including theatricality. Without making one experience exhaustive of reality or normatively prior over others. It's the experience of space which emerges from the baroque period onwards, the theatrical screen, the mirror of the soul and its devices, that allow us to express the world and its relation to others in it in terms that invite comparison with older image-systems and devices that permit a participatory experience. For example, dark glasses and obsidian mirrors can be brought together with the black mirrors of our smartphone screens as creative of the inscrutable and inaccessible image that invites a great deal of participation and completion, as in call-and-response formats common to black music, writerly poetry and videogames. These are distillations of a general dialectic of concealment and revelation that isn't culturally or identity-specific but specific to the site of the encounter between Christian Europeans and Amerindians less prone to believing in belief from the baroque period onwards. Such dialectic is also the creative space of the public, with political implications. Think of that space as the abarian point between two field forces, or even more. A point which is crucial to plot one's motion between worlds such as the Earth and the Moon or the skies above and the underground. In modern times this means to take seriously the question that comes to us from the literatures of supposedly pre-theatrical times: can we move backwards or downwards looking forwards? Or the same: is there such a thing as an open future, for example a future without mirror-souls or screens? The screen isn't just a technological innovation or a man-made clever device, but the object we can use to think about the experience of the animated word as a key ingredient in a specific organisation of time and space. And by extension, of memory. Specific encounters in which part of the fiction is that there is no fiction, that there is no screen there. This in no way means that presence is a thing of the "primitive" past.

It persists in the shape of a cave, the underground and the experience of the underground we have had while following Hu girl and Ix through their katabasis. An experience that is basic to the telling of stories, to the extent that it may be the elemental medium of poetry and story itself. Only that the moments of ecstasy, immediacy, impacting action or the abarian moments are couched in, happen in, and become present to us from within the confines of the cave and the underground. Which is to say that our very desire for the cave is theatrical, as inherent to the life of the word as it is of our drive to and away from death. Persistence of theatre, then. And persistence of presence. "And," not "or." There's no need to up our words with performativity because the latter is internal to our language, an effect of theatre and of presence peering to us through the fourth wall, not outside of it. There's no outside of the fourth wall. And that is why we can look at the lens of the camera. The take won't be rubbish.

Sound-specific prose poem, or not

Words tend to be regarded nowadays as needing help, embellishment, photoshop, and make up. And are, therefore, presumed ugly, decrepit or even death if left on their own. They are condemned and damned. Poor words uttered by poorer people, the stupid masses that simply are. Better, then, to leave important matters to important people. The masters of the universe, who can perform better. Our current lords and heroes (yes, we can be heroes too, but as Bowie said, just for one day). Me, I can't perform. This I said when I was asked to perform as part of the Spoken Word Festival in Southbank. I know, perhaps it was one of those hinging moments when destiny catches up. Life or Death. I know, I was arrogant, paraphrasing Nathaniel Mackey and Wilson Harris that way, rolling them into one without proper credits. But what can I say? I'm just a bookish poet, a writerly one. And writerly poets are bothered by the word performance. Writerly poets are advocates of the animated word; devotees of what shamans call the inner life of the word. Meaning it can create imaginary domains and theatrical spaces. These can be mapped. One such mapping shows that there is an extensive "sound geography" along the Northwest Amazon border of Brazil, Venezuela, and Colombia that consists of crucial locations, borders and thresholds, of creolised Arawakan, Akan, and other invention traditions. This includes waterfalls with petroglyphs and stone formations in which the wind composes whispers and whistles that suggest to the ear (patient enough to learn how to listen) the beginning of the universe at the Hipana rapids, the first death, and its rebirth through the underground quest and rebirth of the twins (like Hu and Ix). This sound geography and the elements of story found in it simply point to a broader sense of reciprocity and responsibility for the structures that hold together a material world – which we seehear as patterns that not only exist but must be continuously animated & preserved. It is said that those who came before us left traces of their presence at these sites, as fragments or ruins of memories, and it is up to us to re-make them. These sites are thresholds or portals. They are positioned not only in space but also in time. Let us use the term *mythscape* to refer to the large landscape in which such thresholds can be found. A comparable notion may be the "Dreamtime" of the Aborigenes of Australia. My journey as Hu made it possible to plot a mythscape map. It contains:

(1) Hipana, as the birthplace of the universe, of humanity, and of Kuwai, also known as Ix -a living being figured as a set of flutes & trumpets engaged in a sort of jazz improv.
(2) A rapids slightly downriver from Hipana, which is the emergence site of the group my abuela came from, located in the upper Guainia River around the town of Maroa. It is the responsibility of the palabrero wordsmiths who reside there to guard the rapids from destruction or defilement such as can be brought by miners and settlers who often pawn their lives to the Lords of Death and the paramilitary led by Señor Matanza. They ensure that everyone who visits can see, hear, and learn from the sound beats of the boulders and petroglyphs, one of which shows the "false Kuwai", the Lords of Death, and the trials they put the twins through: the "pain of the whip", a "sieve for filtering manioc" or a mirror-soul, and spirals making present "sounds of flutes" coming from under the ground.
(3) Nearby, in Uaracapory, on the upper Vaupés, is the site of the Great Tree of Sustenance, which existed at the time of the First Universe. When the Great Tree was cut down, humanity obtained food for their gardens and the wordsmiths, pajés, and shamans gained their storytelling

powers. Look for them in the poetry of Alejandro
Jodorowsky and René Ménil or Suzanne Césaire. Sorry,
I'm at it again. An arrogant fool dropping names, again.

The thing is, when you asked me to perform poetry for
ladies and lords, I found that word most inconvenient
and bothersome. What did you expect? My abuela was a
Colombian living in the UK. After the fall, I grew up in a
doomeddomed Council Estate in ExLondon. She would tell
me the stories of Maroa and Uaracapory, of the Great Tree
of Sustenance and the place they called The Garden. She
spoke of guerrillas turning into bulls to get the conservative
militias at night. She told me about my father's library. So,
I turned up a pedantic arsehole, reading fantasy tales to my
sisters and my friends. After the Church Council banned
them, I would hide a few inside the dolls abuela helped me
put together, sawn from discarded parts in the manner of
monsters. She taught me how to deal with mythic matter,
dark matter, and other deviant substances. She was shaman,
or wordsmith. She pretended to be, if you prefer, so she
could make a buck or two selling liquids, psychedelics, and
shit. I learned from her. I learned hard and I learned it fast.
She said I was her enforcer, retribution, and vengeance.
Lady Justice. Small wonder, they sent their moral police,
their inquisitors and witches after me. I was just a girl. I
had no other choice than running and returning. And run
and turn and return is all I have done. I convinced some
smuggler friends to get my sis and I out of town in one of
those DIY sub-boats dealers use to cross the channel into
war-torn Europe. During the crossing, a witch got to us.
They hate us. They wanted to kill us, break us. They took
everyone and left me for dead. No mirror, no ID, no name.
They took my sis too. I must have spent weeks stranded
at sea. Until I made it here. Wherever here is. Other side

of the ocean, between the Caribbean and the Anaconda River. Carried by the Gulf Stream, I guess, even though they say it collapsed many years ago. The AMOC global conveyor belt. Turns out climate meltdown was non-linear. We didn't know what degrees of warming will cause what aspects of the Earth-system to go bunkers. It did. Half the world drowned. The other half were cooked alive. So, here I was, at the entrance of a tall edifice part of which was immersed between the Caribbean Sea and the Orinoco River. It looked like a cave. The men guarding the entrance had damaged skin, scorpion-red. One of them comes to us, *to eat as if flesh of the gods*, they said. *Two thirds goddess, the rest badass*, I replied. Why have you come on such a long journey? I'm looking for a place called The Garden. I'm on a salvage operation to rescue the elements of story. Ah, you're looking for Utnapishtim. He built himself a boat and was spared by the deluge. People around here think the gods gave him life everlasting. He has plenty of stories to tell. He's on the last floor of this edifice. But there are many floors in this building, many leagues to walk from undercity to topside, and it's all dark. No light in there, and the heat is oppressive, people fall under with solitude and sadness. A desolate place. I entered. I did. When I had travelled one league the darkness became so thick, I could see nothing behind me and nothing ahead of me. Fever struck me after six leagues, and there was like a fog in my mind. My memory is not good because of that. Not factual, unreliable, so I didn't know how to go back and recalled only fragments. Vague images of my dead mother, my escape, a lost sis or a lover. It's all like a spectre haunting. At the end of twelve floors or leagues a boy found me. He shined in my eyes as if the sun itself were streaming in or a star ascended a stare when I shut my eyelids. He claimed to have been a girl once and was about the same age as my lost sister. Perhaps I rolled them into one. He became my brothersister, my lover. We got each other, stood by each other while transiting this dark, awful place. Then, you came. You claimed to be the lord of this land. You came to us saying we were robbers. We were hungry, so we stole your food. We were thirsty, so we took your water. We smelled bad, so we took your flowers, made perfumes, and bathed in them. We cleansed ourselves. You came to us saying we were robbers, pirates. But we have taken these things as gifts nature offers and presented gifts to the mother to express our thanks. The way abuela had taught me. How could we know you claimed property over them? And what if you did? After all, all things are common luxury. Your republic and borders look small when compared to our universal republic. Not to mention the extent of the disaster in here or out there. All things are common luxury. Fruits grew on trees, first. Maize seeds grow in the fields, which abuela taught me how to grind to make cornbread. The water, and the flowers floating in it. You put us on trial. To break us and kill us because you hate us. Because I'm blck. We played your game. The black woman sang. We renamed ourselves. I was Hu. My sis was Ix. You outed us through videodrome, cut us in the house of knives, froze us in the house of cold ice and scolded our feet in fire. In the house of the jaguars, a vampire-like repo man took my head as payment for our debts. Music and the birds who sing bass brought me back when I thought I had lost my mind. Now here I am. You and the other lords said *perform, embrace the deadness of the word as your inner wound*. Because I'm a girl you say I have an inner wound. But I'm writerly dancer and poet too. For me there's no performance. It is not me performing, it's the words on the page and the sounds in the air that do. And it is the words and the sounds that will defeat you.

Light My Fire

Embracing each other
Hu and Ix bowed their heads to the earth
and exploded precipitating a fire.
They died together.

The Lords of Xibalbá
called Xulú and Pacam at once.
We did it
We hated them so we broke them and killed them.
What must we do with their bones?
The blind prophet and his deaf companion performed the rites of divination and
told the lords to grind them and throw them into the river.

But the mother bones did not go very far.
Flowing all the way to the bottom they transformed into bright young girls.
Their faces glowing like the sun and the moon themselves.

Do not ask how long is an instant
or a second
Do not ask to measure with forensic precision its succession
or to calculate its length and duration
for the moment you ask that
is the moment of your fall and ruin
you will mistake a perfect solid for reality
the inquisition's fantasies for fantasies
and miss all that flows, transit, and transforms.

Here they come.
In flow,
Transit,
and transformed.
The twins
Hu and Ix
Reborn.
On their backs,
They bring sunlight.
Time.
And stories.
As old as time.

Epilogue

Post-expectant Futurity.

We stand on lost
loose
oddly elevated ground, the
apotheosis of war
in the lands of our childhood.

This is no glib-materialisation
of loss or fabricated sound, the
anti-expectant gist of which is
what the prophet warned us about.

That 'post' might turn out
to be 'premature'.

Not be what it wanted to be
not post but oddly elevated underground, the
ingenious outdoing of disingenuously harboured hopes
of post-expectant futurity.

Noise or atomistic l/edge
of post-expectant futures running aground, the
multiply-possessed before body before we hit
the ground running into full mediation without reference to
the original body
a single note or primary self.

Even though its multiply-pinned message
gave an operatic lift to the post-expectant ground, the
quantum-qualitative nonsense sound of cyberpunk prophets

dreaming of the network gridling the globe as a nascent life-
form or absolute spirit

but it is lost loose ground, another let there be light ground
and goad rolled into one

Part seismic spirit, part alternate voice
like Movement 4 of Floating Points moving around, the
auto-inscriptive lilt a theatre to not coin a phrase
inasmuch as what we want is real.

What this meant was that want
walked with real across fantastic grounds, the
ripped-ruptural affirmation of post-expectant promises,
premises, and premonitions
running thru it all rolled into one.

The odd post-expectant way it had
of rolling promise, premise, and premonition round into
one, the
whole piece into one piece
into one mixed-metaphorical sound not ground.

Here we stand if stand could be said
what we did when we went underground, the
clubs in which we played on decks mixed-metaphorical sounds

conveyor-belt
carpet-ride
mist-pointillist plank
splint low-lying spray

of post-expectant futurity

and dance

not tragedy.

Political Poetry of the Future

This is a rhythmic overlay
between
Qhipnayra uñtasis sarnaqapxañani
and
the meticulous realisation of our dream's desire.

I

A bass-soaked overlay
reverb saturates,
the line of succession
and
temporal orientation
towards an apocalyptic end.
It opens an interval in timespace.

II

The lowest rhythmic interval
becoming music or wave.
An axion mass scale wave.
It acts
sometimes
as if made of billiard-ball parts
and other times
sloshing like watery waves.
Waves coming together in rhythmic overlay
to create a super wave
that no archive can place
in a final resting place.

III

The revolution will not be televised, he said.
But our protest will be sampled.
A bass-soaked overlay
That reverb saturates
Black matter
opening
La frontera border en el fin.
A void vortex,
an open wound.

IV

Heridas abiertas
con
Venas abiertas
And void vórtices
Vorágine verde y hojarasca
A leaf storm's shocking return, in
whirlpools of water
from where everything comes
to which everything returns
for there's no loss
No beginning
No end
But
base suspense,
bass-soaked relay
outside of today's visual array.

V

Consider the power of words in the age of self-image:

'US-headquartered companies bought the
rights
to water in other countries.'
South of the border.
'These companies are
strangers to the gods of those waters, were
not
formed from them, have never said Gracias
to
those waters, never prayed to those waters
have never been cleansed by those waters.'[16]
Is there any chance the gods may come back angry?

VI

That is why we protest.
Not the human we
are not.
But
The thirst protests.
The hunger protests.
The lack of air protests.
That is why we protest.
We know
The revolution will not be televised,
But the protest will be sampled.
Cut-up, cut-in, and overlayed, intervals between imaginals
Or
Rhythmic sound overlays
to
seehear

---

[16] Natalie Diaz, Postcolonial Love Poem (London: Faber & Faber, 2020) 70.

and
sensethink
Not to contemplate
But to dance
& axion.

VII

Therefore
no wonder
and
no fear
but word cinemas,
dwelling,
rambling
wandering
We trans move
Looking forwards
Moving backwards
Backwards
 we dancewalk
Searching in futures past for light
of what is to come
but not yet.
We walk
Together
In alliance
without allegiance
Rhythm wise
but not straight
In bass-soaked intervals
Until we reach the crossroads
where the old has died but hangs on zombie-like
and the new wants to be born

But not yet.

VIII

Here the future begins,
back to the heart
back to the womb
back to the matter
of futures past
which never stop
if we stop
thinking metamerically,
we may distinguish
diametrically
 vertiginously
The light of lighthouses
From the lanterns of wreckers
wishing to lure us aground
to loot us
and slave us.

IX

We may not want to know it
But we can't shake it off
The feeling
that
We must break free from these chains.
Shed this body.
For it is not so much that the body is a kind of clothing,
But clothing which is a kind of body.
It as the poet says:
'Take my body and make of it–

A Nation.'[17]
But one without confession
Or allegiance.
For it assumes the homogenous body of a Nation.
'An American way of forgetting Natives.
Discover them with City. Crumble them by
City.
Erase them into Cities named for their
Bones, until
You are the new Natives of your new Cities …
[But] Who lies beneath [these] streets, [these] universities,
[these] art
Museums?'[18]
She asks.

X

Let's cross the border in the opposite direction.
Go south
at sea
to see
really see
dance
& seehear
A rhythmic overlay
A bass-soaked relay
That reverb saturates without delay
For we can no longer wait.

---

[17] Natalie Diaz, Postcolonial Love Poem, 56.

[18] Natalie Diaz, Postcolonial Love Poem, 64.